Parents and Caregivers,

Stone Arch Readers are designed to provide enjoyable reading experiences, as well as opportunities to develop vocabulary, literacy skills, and comprehension. Here are a few ways to support your beginning reader:

- Talk with your child about the ideas addressed in the story.

- Discuss each illustration, mentioning the characters, where they are, and what they are doing.

- Read with expression, pointing to each word. You may want to read the whole story through and then revisit parts of the story to ensure that the meanings of words or phrases are understood.

- Talk about why the character did what he or she did and what your child would do in that situation.

- Help your child connect with characters and events in the story.

Remember, reading with your child should be fun, not forced. Each moment spent reading with your child is a priceless investment in his or her literacy life.

Gail Saunders-Smith, Ph.D.

Stone Arch Readers

are published by Stone Arch Books
a Capstone Imprint
1710 Roe Crest Drive
North Mankato, Minnesota 56003
www.capstonepub.com

Library of Congress Cataloging-in-Publication Data
Klein, Adria F. (Adria Fay), 1947-
  Hank Hammer and the puppy / by Adria Klein ; illustrated by Andrew Rowland.
      p. cm. -- (Stone Arch readers--tool school)
  Summary: Hank Hammer and the Tool Team build a doghouse for his new puppy.
  ISBN 978-1-4342-4020-0 (library binding) -- ISBN 978-1-4342-4233-4 (pbk.)
 1. Hammers--Juvenile fiction. 2. Puppies--Juvenile fiction. 3. Doghouses--Juvenile fiction.
4. Tools--Juvenile fiction. 5. Helping behavior--Juvenile fiction. [1. Hammers--Fiction. 2. Dogs-
-Fiction. 3. Doghouses--Fiction. 4. Tools--Fiction. 5. Helpfulness--Fiction.] I. Rowland, Andrew,
1962- ill. II. Title.

  PZ7.K678324Hap 2012
  [E]--dc23

                              2011049283

Reading Consultants:
Gail Saunders-Smith, Ph.D.
Melinda Melton Crow, M.Ed.
Laurie K. Holland, Media Specialist

Designer: Russell Griesmer

Printed in China
032012
006677RRDF12

Hank
Hammer
and the Puppy

by Adria Klein   illustrated by Andy Rowland

MEET THE
TOOL
TEAM

Tia Tape Measure

5
4
3
2
1

floor section

Hank Hammer

8 × 14"

Sammy Saw

Sophie Screwdriver

Hank has some exciting news.
He can't wait to tell his friends!

"They'll be here soon,"
says his mom.

Hank sees his friends and runs outside.

"What's going on?" asks Sammy.

"We have a new member to add to our group," says Hank.

"Who is it?" asks Tia.

"It's my new puppy!" says Hank.
"His name is Happy."

"Wow!" says Sophie. "You are so lucky!"

"Where does he sleep?" asks Sammy.

"I don't have a place for Happy to sleep," says Hank.

"Happy needs a doghouse,"
says Tia.

"He sure does!" says Sophie.

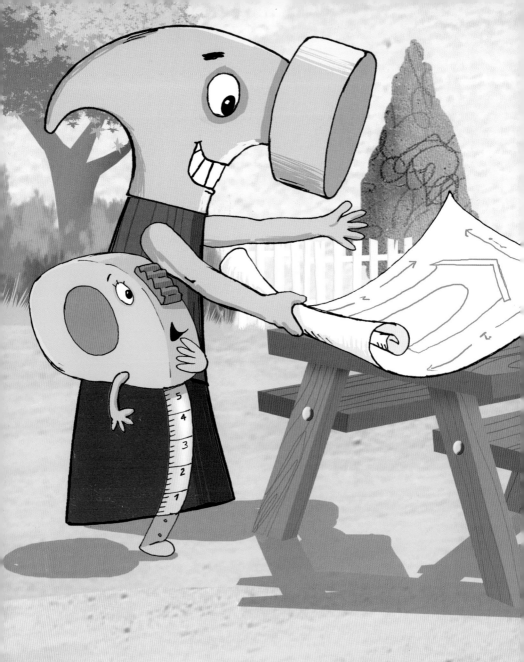

"Let's get to work," says Hank.

"First, we need a plan," says Sammy.

"Like this?" asks Hank.

"Yes! You always have a plan," says Sammy.

"I can measure the wood," says Tia.

"I can saw the wood," says Sammy.

"I can hold the wood,"
says Sophie.

"And I can hammer the wood
together," says Hank.

"Let's do this, Tool Team!"
says Hank.

Hank gets the wood. Sammy
and Sophie get the nails. Tia
gets the paint.

Tia measures each piece of wood.
Sammy cuts each piece of wood.

Hank and Tia play with Happy.

"We're done with our part," says Tia.

"Your turn," says Sammy.

"I'm ready," says Hank.

"So am I," says Sophie.

Sophie holds the wood. Hank
hammers and hammers.

Tia and Sammy play with Happy.

"Now we need to paint the doghouse," says Hank.

"We can all do that!" says Sophie.

"Now I can hang the sign," says
Hank. "The doghouse is done."

"Good work, Tool Team! I think
Happy likes his new house,"
says Hank's mom.

"I think he does," says Hank.

"Time for a picture," says his mom.
"Smile!"

Now everyone is happy.

STONE ARCH READERS 2

TOOL SCHOOL

Tia Tape Measure
and the Move

by Adria Klein
illustrated by Andy Rowland

STONE ARCH READERS 2

TOOL SCHOOL

Sammy Saw
and the Campout

by Adria Klein
illustrated by Andy Rowland

STONE ARCH READERS 2

TOOL SCHOOL

Sophie Screwdriver
and the Classroom

by Adria Klein
illustrated by Andy Rowland

TOOL SCHOOL